Happy Belly, Happy Smile

RACHEL ISADORA

Harcourt Children's Books

Houghton Mifflin Harcourt

Boston   New York   2009

Friday is my favorite day.
On Fridays I have dinner
with Grandpa Sam.
He owns a restaurant
in Chinatown.

There is a big fish tank in the window,
and everyone stops to look.

"Hi, Louie!" says Dan the waiter
when we come in.
Everyone is very busy eating.

In the kitchen
I say hello to Chef Ben.
There is so much steam,
I can hardly see him.
"Hi, Louie—is that you?" he says.

David is busy rolling egg rolls.
Liang is peeling shrimp.

I like to watch Chef Lee chop vegetables.
His hands move so fast.

Suddenly Jai rushes in. "Delivery pickup!"
He takes the bags and puts them on his bicycle
and then rides away.
"He even delivers in the pouring rain!" Liang says.

"Where are the spareribs
for table eight?"
calls Dan from the door.
"They're on their way!" another waiter shouts back.

"Time to eat," Grandpa Sam says.

"I'm hungry."

"Me too," I say.

We sit at a table under the paper dragon,
which Grandpa says brings good luck.

I see my friend.
"Hey, Franklin!" I say.

"This is my favorite food,"
he tells me.
"Cool!" I say. "Me too!"

My grandpa and I eat with chopsticks,
but most of the time at home I use
a fork, knife, and spoon.

The waiter brings a big bowl of rice.
He brings steamed dumplings, egg rolls,
and shrimp chow mein.
My favorite.

Grandpa orders a fish.

"No, thank you, Grandpa!"

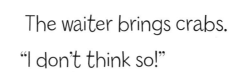

The waiter brings crabs.

"I don't think so!"

At the end of dinner, Grandpa gives me
a fortune cookie. I open it up
and Grandpa reads, "Happy food,
happy belly, happy smile."
Then the waiter puts a dish
of orange slices on the table.
I go over to Franklin, and he turns around.

Grandpa laughs.

"Now, that's what I call a happy smile!"

For Lee and Hy Simon

Printed in Singapore
Harcourt Children's Books is an imprint of Houghton Mifflin Harcourt Publishing Company.
www.hmhbooks.com
The illustrations in this book were done in collage and oil on palette paper.

Library of Congress Cataloging-in-Publication Data
Isadora, Rachel.
Happy belly, happy smile / Rachel Isadora.
p. cm.
Summary: Sitting in the kitchen of his grandfather's Chinese restaurant, a young boy enjoys watching the chefs and waiters prepare and serve mouth-watering dishes.
ISBN 978-0-15-206546-1
[1. Restaurants—Fiction. 2. Chinese Americans—Fiction. 3. Grandfathers—Fiction.] I. Title.
PZ7.I763Hap 2009
[E]—dc22
2008046221

TWP 10 9 8 7 6 5 4 3 2 1

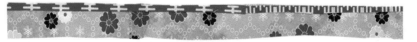

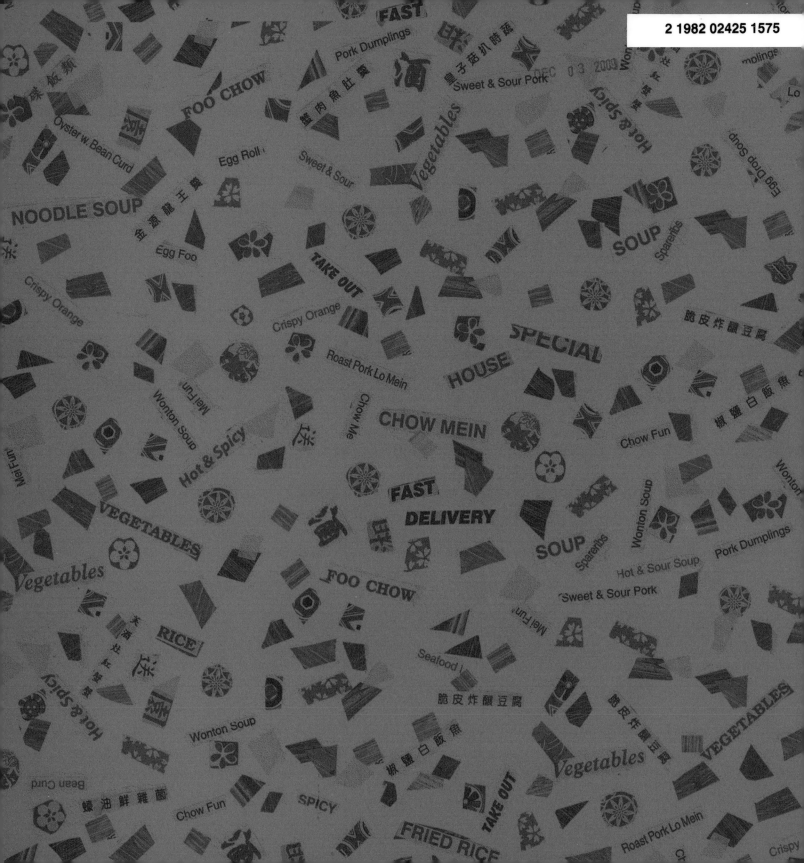